Nurse Nancy

By KATHRYN JACKSON

Pictures by
CORINNE MALVERN

 A GOLDEN BOOK • NEW YORK

Educators and librarians, for a variety of teaching tools, visit us at
www.randomhouse.com/teachers
Library of Congress Control Number: 2004105523
ISBN: 978-0-375-83262-8
Printed in the United States of America
20 19 18 17 16 15 14

NANCY liked to play with dolls.
She liked to play Mother. She liked to play
Teacher. And best of all, she liked to play Nurse.

She had a fine doll hospital, complete with lots of bandages and handy candy pills.

But she had no one to play with her.

Her brothers called "Nurse Nancy!" as they raced past her door. But they never had time to stop and play. They were always too busy with big boy games.

Mother stopped in at the hospital sometimes.
One day, she had a hurt finger.
Down from her shelf Nurse Nancy took a brand-new box.
And she put on Mother's finger a red, heart-shaped plastic bandage.

Another day, Nancy heard a great commotion out in the back yard.

It didn't sound like just a lively baseball game. It sounded like trouble. And it was!

The boys' ball had hit a bees' nest, and angry bees
were pouring out.

"Look out!" Tom shouted. "Here they come!" And the three boys came racing toward the house, with the angry bees close behind.

Nancy ran and held the door open while the boys
came piling in. Then she slammed it shut on the bees.
"Whew!" panted the boys. "We are safe!"

But Tom was not safe. He had fallen.
Nancy was a nurse, so Nancy knew what to do.
First she took a good look at the wound.

She got a clean cloth and a towel from the drawer. She dampened and soaped the cloth. "Go and lie down, patient," she said.

Tom did, and she propped a pillow under his leg,
with a clean towel over the top.
Then she washed that cut off carefully.
"It's clean now," Nancy said.

The damp cloth was nice and cool against the burning sting. Soon the hurt had stopped.

"How do you feel now?" Nancy asked.

"Much better," said Tom, and he tried to smile. But when he looked at the ugly cut, he could not quite manage a smile.

"I can fix that," said Nancy. So she opened her
supply box and covered the cut with a brightly
colored bandage.

That brand-new bandage looked so fresh and fine
that even Tom could smile at it now.

When Mother came home, the boys told her all
about the cut and Nurse Nancy's good care, while
they had their lunch.

"I'm proud of you, dear," said Mother. And she
gave Nancy a special hug and an extra cookie, too.

After lunch the boys hung around instead of
hurrying back out to play.

"What do you say we play ambulance?" Billy
suggested.

"Fine," said Nancy.

So they fixed up the wagon for an ambulance.

Just then, ding-a-ling, came a telephone ring.
Nurse Nancy answered.

"Hospital," she said.

"There's been an accident," she heard a voice call.
"Down at the big tree."

They all looked down there, just in time to see
Billy flopping down, moaning fine big moans.
"I'll drive the ambulance," Tom cried.
"I'll be the doctor," cried Dan.

Then away they raced! Tom pulled the ambulance.
Doctor Dan raced beside him, with his doctor bag.
And Nurse Nancy proudly rode.

When they reached the accident, Nurse Nancy
put a bandage on Billy for first aid.

Then the doctor and the ambulance man lifted
him onto the ambulance, and back to the hospital
they went.

Billy had such a good time playing sick, with pink
and green candy pills, that the others could hardly
wait for their turns.

The telephone kept ringing with ambulance calls, patients kept coming to the hospital wanting brand-new bandages. Nurse Nancy was so busy she could scarcely think.

"Well," she said, when supper time came to end her busy day, "I'm certainly glad I'm a nurse!"